THREAT PLANET

written by Tony Juniper
illustrated by Simone Boni, Lorenzo Cecchi *and* Ivan Stalio

Ladybird

CONTENTS

SPACESHIP EARTH

Billions of stars are scattered through the darkness of space. Some are seen at night as pinpricks of light. Many stars have planets, but only the Earth is known to have life. Stable temperatures, oxygen and plenty of water have brought millions of different animals and plants to life.

The Sun

The Sun is the closest star to Earth – about 150 million kilometres away. Without the Sun's energy there would be no life on Earth.

Stars

Stars are made from gases that produce tremendous heat and light. A large cluster of stars is called a galaxy. Light from some stars takes so long to reach the Earth that although the star appears to be shining in the sky, it may no longer exist.

LIFE ON EARTH

The Earth was formed about 4,000 million years ago. About 3,000 million years ago, the earliest forms of life appeared. The process of development which has continued since then is called **evolution**. This usually occurs slowly, taking place over millions of years. The Earth is probably home to about thirteen or fourteen million different **species** – no one knows the exact number.

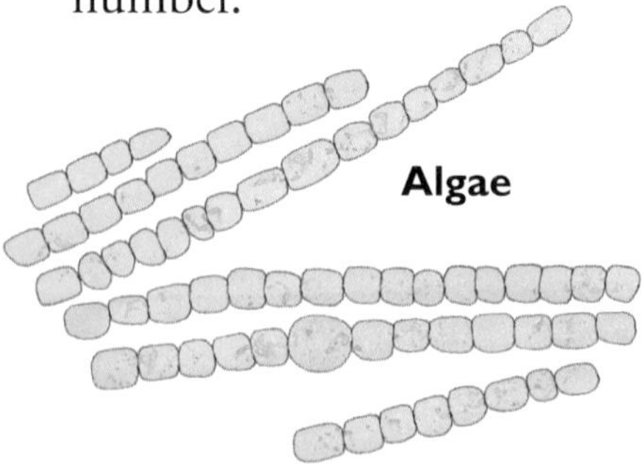

Algae

The first life
The first life forms were very simple. They were bacteria and very small algae, which can only be seen with a microscope.

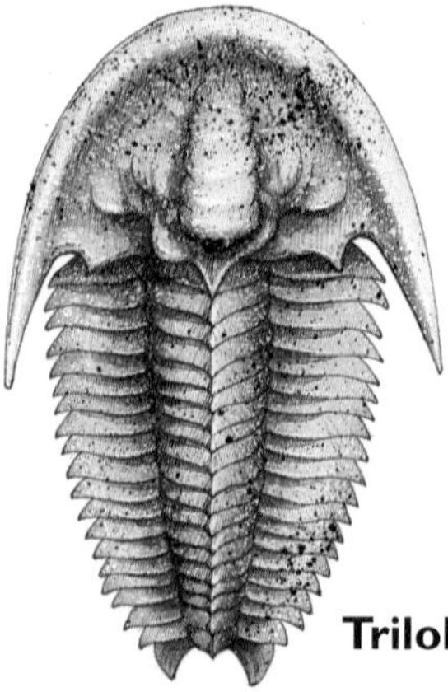

Shelled sea animals
By about 600 million years ago, larger creatures had evolved in the seas. These were soft-bodied worms, jellyfish and animals with shells, like the trilobite. The first fish followed later.

Trilobite

Land animals
About 300 million years ago, animals with backbones first appeared on land. Millions of years later, they evolved into reptiles, like the eryops.

Eryops

Mammals and birds

These groups have only developed over about the past 150 million years. The first bird, called *Archaeopteryx*, is thought to be related to the dinosaurs. The earliest **mammals** were tiny creatures, a bit like mice in appearance.

The first people

The first people are thought to have evolved from apes about three million years ago. They lived by hunting animals and gathering plants.

Much later on, people spread across the world and started to settle down. They built houses and made inventions that began to change the whole world.

People today

Today, people are the most widespread form of life. In just a few thousand years people have transformed from being hunter-gatherers to being inventors and users of complex machines like computers, aircraft and spaceships.

PEOPLE AND OUR PLANET

As the number of people on the Earth has grown, so has the need for vast amounts of fuel, food and **natural resources**. Finding and using these things can cause damage to the **environment**, threatening other life forms and even people themselves.

An oil rig

Fuel

Fuel is needed to power vehicles and factories and to heat homes. Most fuels come from the remains of dead plants, trapped millions of years ago in rocks. These are **fossil fuels** and include coal, oil and gas. Most oil and gas is drilled for by rigs and coal is mined on land. Sometimes, forests are cut down so that coal and metals can be mined from under the ground. This activity can change large areas of land.

Cities

Large cities contain millions of people. They all need huge quantities of clean water, food, petrol, electricity and paper. As people use up more and more natural materials, resources become depleted and the environment is more at risk.

Rainforests

Rainforest trees help to keep the balance of the Earth's environment by soaking up water from the soil and releasing it slowly into the atmosphere through their leaves. They also affect **carbon dioxide** levels in the air which, in turn, affects the Earth's climate. These forests stop the soil being washed away by heavy rain and provide homes for millions of different kinds of plants and animals.

Wood

People need wood for many things, such as building homes and making furniture. A lot of the wood we use comes from rainforests. But rainforest trees do not grow quickly enough to meet the demand for wood. Trees are often cut down just to clear the land for farming, but without the trees the soil is washed away and the forest is gone forever. This is known as **deforestation**.

Paper

Newspapers, magazines and writing paper are all made from wood fibres. Huge numbers of trees are needed to provide the world's paper supply.

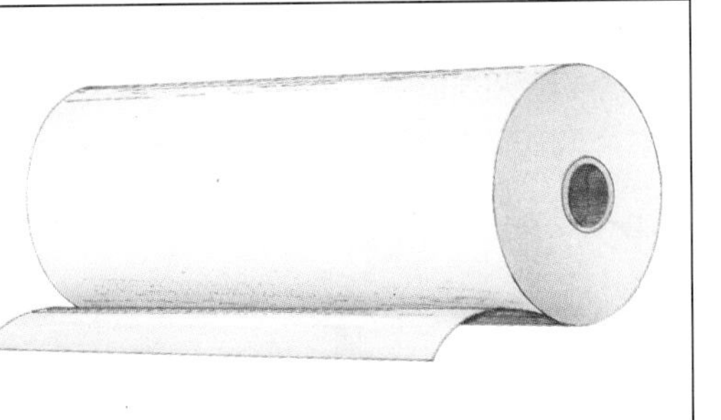

THE GREENHOUSE EFFECT

Most scientists now believe that **pollution** in the air is warming up the Earth's climate. Gases such as carbon dioxide act like a sheet of glass above the Earth trapping the Sun's heat and making the air warmer than usual. This is called the greenhouse effect.

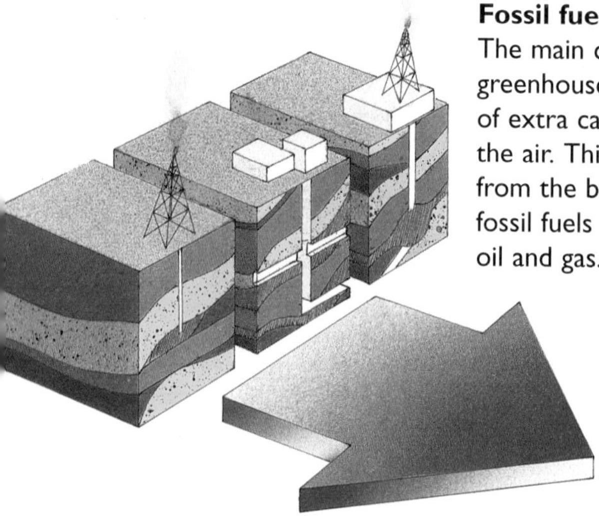

Fossil fuels

The main cause of the greenhouse effect is the release of extra carbon dioxide gas into the air. This gas comes mainly from the burning of fossil fuels like coal, oil and gas.

Power and energy

Fossil fuels are used in many ways. Coal is often burnt in power stations to make electricity. Oil is processed into petrol and diesel to power cars, buses and trains. And gas is piped to homes for cooking and heating.

Forests

Carbon dioxide is also released into the atmosphere when forests are cleared and burnt.

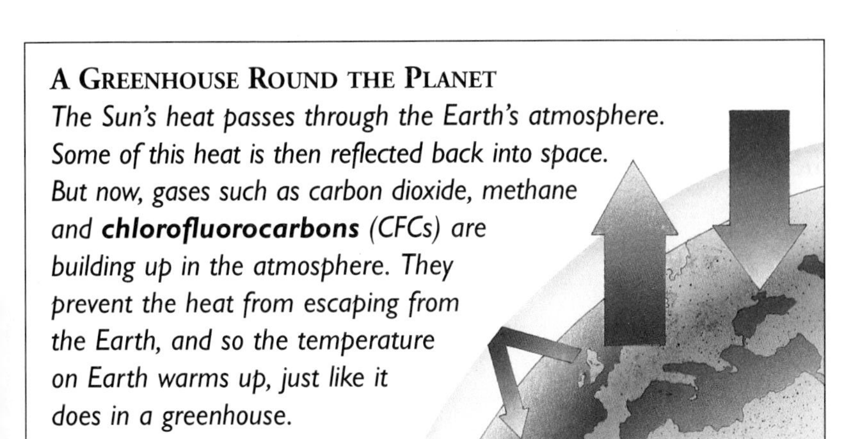

A Greenhouse Round the Planet

The Sun's heat passes through the Earth's atmosphere. Some of this heat is then reflected back into space. But now, gases such as carbon dioxide, methane and **chlorofluorocarbons** *(CFCs) are building up in the atmosphere. They prevent the heat from escaping from the Earth, and so the temperature on Earth warms up, just like it does in a greenhouse.*

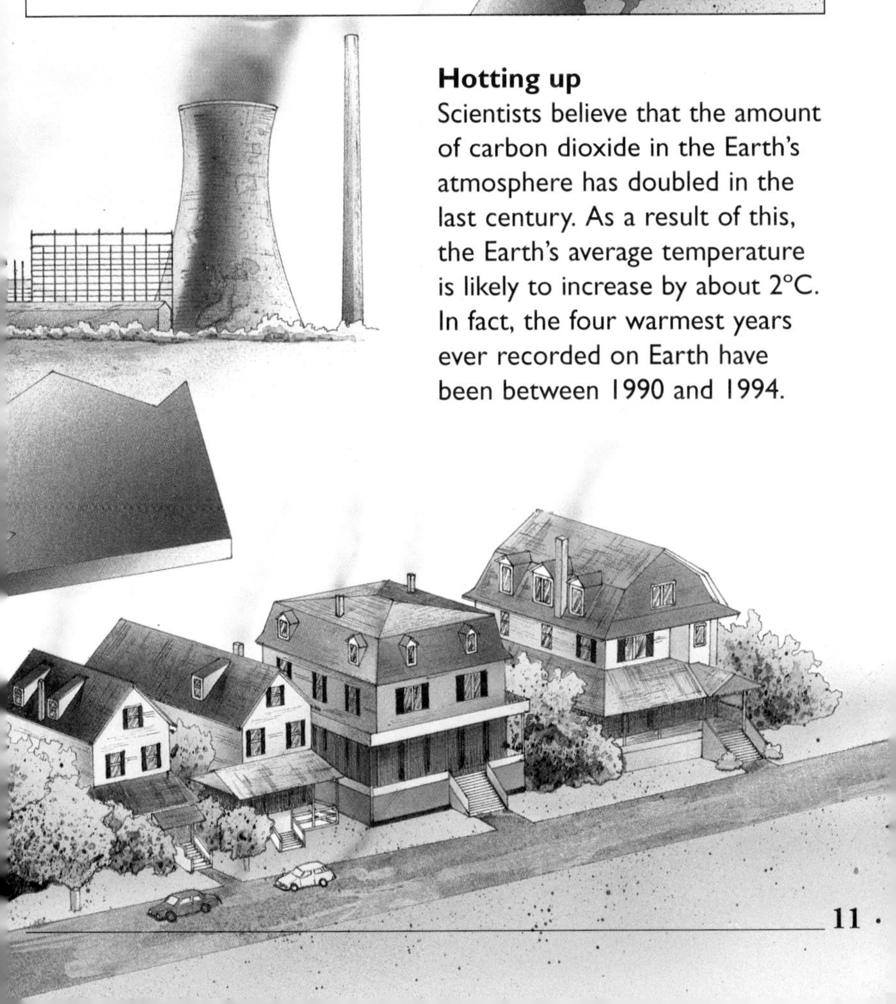

Hotting up

Scientists believe that the amount of carbon dioxide in the Earth's atmosphere has doubled in the last century. As a result of this, the Earth's average temperature is likely to increase by about 2°C. In fact, the four warmest years ever recorded on Earth have been between 1990 and 1994.

THE CHANGING CLIMATE

The greenhouse effect is changing the Earth's climate. Although the climate has changed many times since life first appeared, past changes were much slower than now. This gave plants and animals more time to adapt to new conditions. Rapid climate change, such as is happening now, could threaten many forms of animal and plant life.

Rising seas
As water warms, it expands. As the warming oceans expand, sea levels will rise. Helped by the melting ice, some low lying land will be flooded. No one knows exactly how fast the seas will rise.

The danger of flooding

Changes for wildlife
As the climate changes, the **habitats** of many animals and plants change too. Animals may have to move to other areas where they can live, but plants cannot move in the same way. They will have to adapt to the new conditions or they could die out.

Puffin

Animals in Danger

The threat to animals and plants whose habitats change may not always be obvious. For instance, if there is not enough food for caterpillars, many die from starvation. This will then result in fewer butterflies in the area in the future. Many reptiles are also threatened by global warming. The temperature at which a reptile's egg hatches can affect whether the baby is male or female. A change of just 1°C may result in a shortage of females in some kinds of reptiles. This means that there won't be enough females to ***breed****.*

Food

The greenhouse effect is likely to affect the Earth's weather. Some areas will become warmer and drier, and there may be more storms. This could have serious effects on the world's food production. Areas that are now used for growing crops like rice or wheat might suffer from drought or flooding. They will become less suitable for farming and new areas will be needed.

THE OZONE LAYER

High up in the Earth's atmosphere is a layer of gas called **ozone**. Ozone protects life forms from harmful solar rays that cause cancer in people and damage plant growth. The protective ozone is disappearing because of pollution.

High level shield

Ozone envelopes the Earth in a layer about 25 to 30 kilometres above the ground. New ozone is being made all the time.

Antarctic problem

Ozone loss is a worldwide problem, but it is most serious in Antarctica, where there is a hole in the ozone layer.

Ozone destruction

The ozone layer is in a part of the upper atmosphere called the stratosphere. The ozone layer has been damaged because of chemical gases which have been released into the atmosphere.

Stratosphere

Ozone layer

Chlorofluorocarbons (CFCs)

CFCs are one of the most damaging groups of gases to the ozone layer. They break down and release harmful chlorine into the atmosphere. CFC damage caused today can last for 100 years.

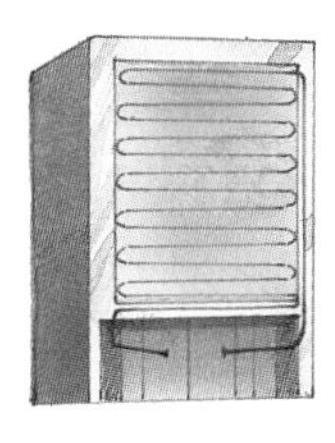

Fridges
Some fridges use CFCs to keep cool. If fridges are thrown away, CFCs can escape into the air.

Pesticides
Methyl bromide is a **pesticide** which destroys ozone 50 times faster than CFCs.

Fire extinguishers
Some types of fire extinguishers contain halon gases. These can be even more damaging than CFCs.

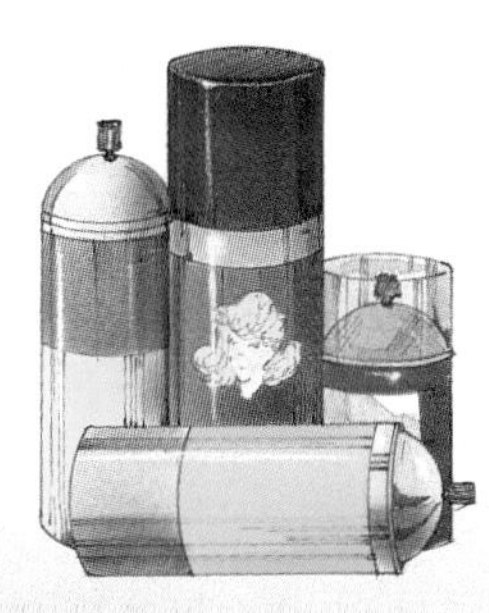

Aerosols
Aerosol sprays used to contain CFCs. Today, many countries do not allow CFCs in aerosols.

SEAFOOD

Because of the reduced ozone in Antarctica, rays from the Sun are entering the sea and slowing the growth of the tiny plants that shrimps and fish feed on. Animals that feed on fish, such as penguins, could suffer food shortages as a result.

MOVING AROUND

All over the world people rely on transport to help run their lives. They need to travel to work, visit friends and go shopping. They also need to move resources, for example, take coal from a mine to a power station. Traditionally, people have used either road vehicles, such as cars, buses and trucks or rail vehicles, like trains and trams. But pollution is produced by many forms of transport, from the fuel that is burnt in the engines.

Catalytic converter

The exhaust fumes from car engines contain many gases which pollute the atmosphere. In recent years, the catalytic converter has been developed. This is a device which is fitted to the exhausts of cars and reduces some types of the pollution that is produced. All new cars now have to be fitted with catalytic converters.

Bikes

Riding a bicycle helps to keep you fit and does not cause any pollution. Cycling on roads can be dangerous, because of the numbers of cars. It could be made safer by building more cycle lanes, where cars aren't allowed.

Trams

People in cities have made efforts to reduce the number of cars on the streets by introducing trams as an alternative way to travel. Trams run on electricity and do not give out as much pollution as cars do. They are also safer to other road users, such as cyclists, because trams run on rails and not all over the road.

Trains

Trains can transport large numbers of people in relation to the pollution they cause. If everyone travelling on a train used a car, the roads would be blocked and the polluting fumes would cause widespread damage to the environment.

SAVING OUR EARTH

Despite all the problems facing the Earth and its environment at the moment there are many things that we can all do to improve the quality of life. Using alternative sources of energy, setting up nature reserves and recycling resources are all practical and positive moves in saving our Earth.

Renewable energy
Natural energy from the Sun, wind and sea can be collected and turned into electricity. This is called renewable energy. It can be cheaper than other forms of energy, doesn't cause pollution and will last forever.

Recycling
When items made from paper, glass, plastic and some metals must be thrown away, recycling is the best way to help save resources, reduce waste and cut pollution. For example, kitchen and garden waste can be made into compost, which is used to improve soil and help plants grow better. Used motor oil from car engines, corks, old clothes and some batteries can all be recycled too.

Friends of the Earth
Friends of the Earth and *Greenpeace* are international organisations that work towards preventing the Earth's natural resources being wasted and the environment spoiled. They try to educate people about the problems facing the Earth today and in the future, and how some of the problems can be avoided. Campaigners spread their ideas using television, newspapers and radio.

Endangered animals
By breeding animals in zoos and then releasing them into the wild, a few endangered creatures might be saved from **extinction**. For example, the European bison became extinct in the wild because of hunting and habitat loss. Bison that had been bred in zoos were released in 1919 and can now be found in a few places in the wild.

Rescued animals
Some birds of prey were wiped out from many areas because of poisonous chemicals sprayed on crops. In the places that the chemicals have been banned, the birds have come back.

THREATENED EARTH

Today the Earth is under threat because we are using its resources too quickly and we do not do enough to prevent pollution of the air, water and land. The growth of industry and transport has brought many benefits but it has also led to a large increase in the levels of pollution.

Traffic
The world's vehicles are a major source of pollution. As the number of vehicles increases, more roads are built to make room for them. Some of these roads cut through countryside or woodland and the wildlife there might be wiped out.

Nuclear pollution
Nuclear power stations make electricity without burning fossil fuels. But radioactive waste is produced which is very dangerous if exposed to humans and wildlife. It must be stored properly, in secure containers. Sometimes nuclear waste leaks from containers, causing major environmental problems.

Industrial pollution
Every year, factories all over the world release millions of tonnes of chemicals into the air which can harm the environment. Some chemicals travel in air and water to cause damage hundreds of kilometres away from where they were released.

ACID RAIN

Harmful gases such as sulphur dioxide are produced by cars, factory chimneys and oil or coal power stations. In the atmosphere, these gases combine with water, to form 'acid rain'. When this falls on the land, trees and other vegetation may be killed, while in ponds and lakes, fish and other aquatic creatures are likely to die. Acid rain may also damage buildings.

Disasters at sea

Large quantities of oil are transported in huge ships called supertankers. Sometimes, during heavy storms these ships crash into rocks on the coastline. If the ship breaks up on the rocks, thousands of tonnes of oil are spilled out into the sea. Because oil floats on water it forms a slick which can be many kilometres wide. Hundreds of birds, fish and other animals die by suffocating or drowning as a result of these oil spills. It can take weeks for the affected area to be cleaned up and much longer for the dead wildlife to be replaced.

WATER POLLUTION

People need water to drink, flush the lavatory and to wash dishes and clothes. Factories use lots of water in making all kinds of products from steel to plastics. But afterwards, unless this dirty water is treated it can make people ill and may kill wildlife.

Treating polluted water
Used water travels out of homes in pipes called sewers. It is cleaned in a sewage treatment works before flowing into a river or sea. Sometimes, untreated water goes back into the sea, causing pollution. Even cleaned water may still contain chemicals that are non-**biodegradable**, and can harm wildlife.

Factory pollution
Many countries have laws to protect water supplies from factory waste. But accidents still occur, and many fish and water animals die as a result.

A LOAD OF RUBBISH

Millions of tonnes of rubbish are thrown away every year. It is very wasteful, particularly as much of this rubbish could be recycled and reused. Having to dispose of this rubbish by burying it in the ground or burning it can be harmful to the environment as well.

Waste
In some countries, people produce huge amounts of waste. Getting rid of it can cause serious problems, especially if the waste is poisonous. Burning waste can cause air pollution and dumping it in the sea could cause water pollution if the containers leak.

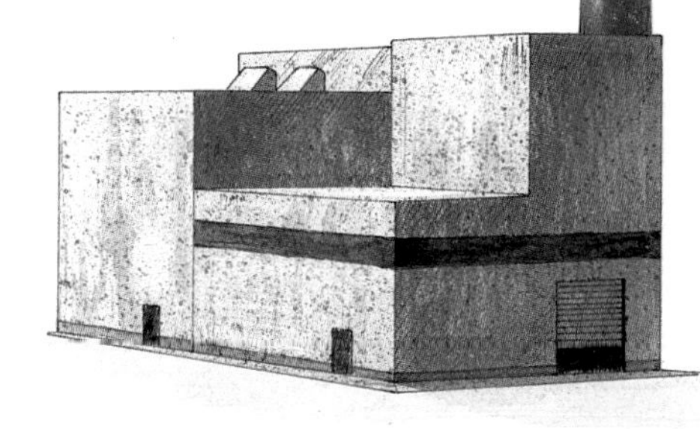

Up in smoke
Because there are fewer places to bury waste, more is being burned in **incinerators**. By using this method, toxic gases can be released into the air and the ash left behind can be poisonous too.

Buried rubbish
Millions of tonnes of rubbish is buried underground. This waste produces poisonous liquids which can enter underground water supplies, polluting people's drinking water.

THE RICH, THE POOR AND THE WORLD

Many of the world's most serious environmental problems are caused by people in the **developed world**. Although only 20 per cent of the world's people live in this part of the world, they use 80 per cent of the world's energy and raw materials. Many people believe that sharing the world's resources more fairly between people is necessary to solve environmental problems.

In this way, the rich would use up less and the poor would be able to meet their needs without destroying valuable local resources.

A different world

It is common for people in the developed world to use water whenever they want to, and they often throw it away when it could be used again.

But one billion of the world's people do not have supplies of clean water. Millions of children become ill and die as a result of this.

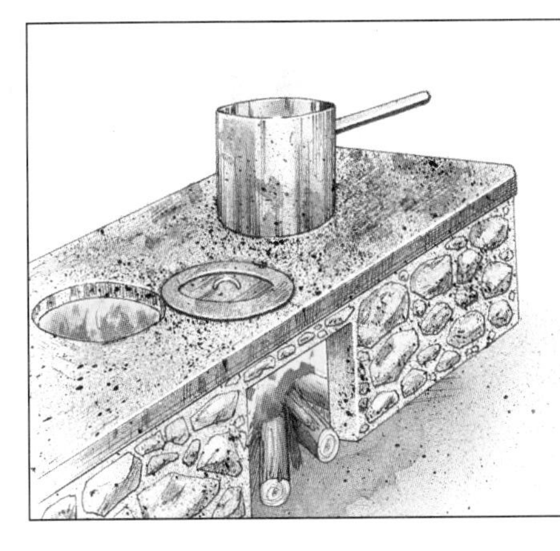

COOKING

People in poor countries use lots of wood to cook their food. To find this wood, they must chop down local trees. If they had more efficient cookers they could use less wood and areas of forest would be saved.

The risk of starvation

If the world's climate changes, people in poorer countries who depend on the land will suffer most. If it does not rain, for example, their crops will not grow, their animals will die through lack of water and the people are likely to starve.

RENEWABLE ENERGY

We can help protect the environment by using less of the Earth's resources. There are ways of producing energy such as electricity other than by burning fuel in power stations.

Solar power

Light and heat from the Sun can be trapped by **solar panels** on house roofs and turned into electricity.

WIND POWER

Windmills can be used to capture energy from the wind and turn it into electricity. Wind farms can be noisy but there are no fuel costs and no pollution.

Bright idea

Energy efficient light bulbs have been developed that use far less electricity than traditional ones. They cost more but save money in the long term because they last much longer.

DESTROYING HOMELANDS

Many important wildlife areas are under constant threat of destruction. Forests, ponds and heathlands are all home to a great variety of plants and animals. If these areas are destroyed some plants and animals may die out.

Farming
Modern intensive farming helps to produce the food needed to feed the world's growing population but it can affect the environment. Pesticides can kill wild animals, and natural woodlands are cleared to make way for fields of crops. Millions of tonnes of oil are needed to power farm machines like combine harvesters.

Ploughing
Wild grasslands are wonderful places for different kinds of flowers, insects and birds to live. All over the world areas like this are being ploughed up to provide land for growing crops.

Drainage
Swamps, bogs and other watery places are called wetlands. They are home to a rich variety of wildlife. Most wetlands have been drained to make way for farms, hotels, factories and houses. The wildlife that lived there has gone.

SAVING RESOURCES

Everyone can help the environment by making things last longer. This saves resources, cuts pollution and reduces waste. It can save money and provide people with new jobs too.

Wood

Beautiful wood is often thrown away or burnt, even when it can be used again. By using wood to make something else we can stop more trees being cut down.

Bags

Baskets are best as they can be used many times before being replaced. Paper bags are thrown away after one use, and plastic bags can be used a few times, but are not biodegradable.

Paper

Using both sides of a sheet of paper is a small but useful way of saving resources.

RECYCLING

Recycling saves natural resources by making new products from old ones. Materials such as paper, glass and metal can all be recycled and made into packaging and containers that are every bit as good as the original.

Recycling centre
In many towns there are now special containers where people can leave bottles and other items for recycling. Lorries then collect this waste and take it to factories.

Home collection
In some towns people don't even need to take their rubbish to recycling centres. Paper, glass and cans simply have to be put outside in boxes for collection.

Glass
Glass can be melted down and made into new bottles and jars.

Cans
Cans are crushed and recycled so the metal can be used again.

Paper
Waste paper can be recycled four or five times before it has to be thrown away.

NATURE RESERVES

Nature reserves are areas of land or water set aside to protect wildlife. Some are very large, covering tens of thousands of square kilometres. These reserves can help prevent rare animals and plants from becoming extinct.

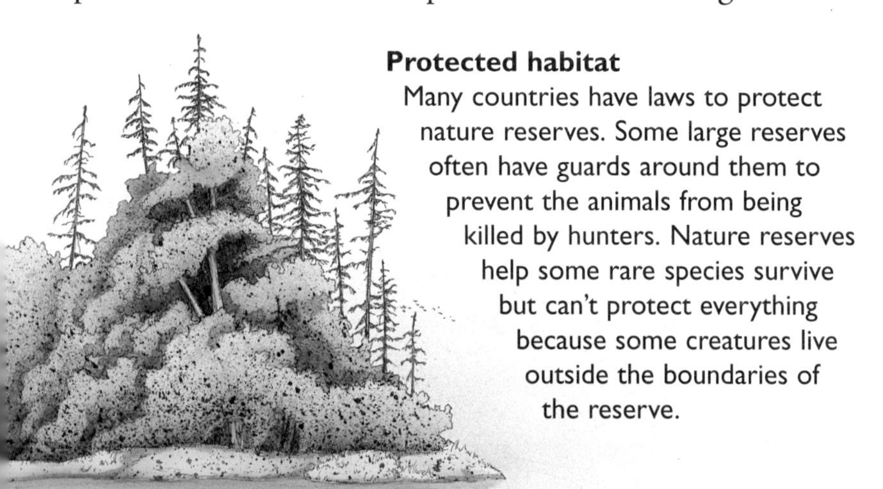

Protected habitat

Many countries have laws to protect nature reserves. Some large reserves often have guards around them to prevent the animals from being killed by hunters. Nature reserves help some rare species survive but can't protect everything because some creatures live outside the boundaries of the reserve.

City wildlife

Nature reserves can be set up in towns and cities too. They are usually quite small but can be ideal places to see many wild animals and plants without travelling to the countryside. City nature reserves can give people a chance to see species that are quite rare in the wild.

FUTURE FORESTS

Forests are vital to us, not just as a source of wood, but also because they affect the world's climate. Many areas of forest are now carefully managed to make sure new trees are planted every time old trees are cut down.

Good wood

Wood from managed or **sustainable forests** sometimes carries a label to say this. If we only buy wood that has these labels we can help forests and their wildlife survive.

AMAZING THREATENED PLANET FACTS

- **Forest destruction** About half of the world's tropical rainforests have been cut down since the 1940s. Every year another 160,000 square kilometres of tropical forest is cleared. This area is larger than England and Wales put together.

- **Today's technology** The light bulbs that were used in the 1920s used 100 times more electricity than the energy efficient bulbs that are in use today.

- **Who uses what?** In India, each person uses an average of 300 litres of petrol per year. In America, each person uses up 7,600 litres. That's about 25 times as much.

- **Oil boom** In the 1990s, the world used about fifteen times more oil every year than was used at the end of the 1940s. Present oil consumption is taking place one million times faster than new oil is being made.

- **Can savings** Aluminium made from recycled cans uses only one twentieth of the energy needed to make new aluminium.

- **Waste production** Industrial activity in America produces about 250 million tonnes of poisonous waste every year. That's equivalent to one tonne of toxic waste for every person who lives there.

- **Species loss** Up to 75 species of animal and plant are becoming extinct every day. That adds up to over 27,000 every year. The main reason for these extinctions is tropical forest destruction.

- **People all over the world** In 1950 there were about two and a half billion people in the world. By 2025 it is estimated that there will be about eight and a half billion.

GLOSSARY

Biodegradable Able to be broken down into tiny harmless products by decay.

Breed To produce offspring.

Carbon dioxide A gas in the air that is very important to the environment.

Chlorofluorocarbons A group of gases that damage the ozone layer.

Deforestation The removal of trees causing the disappearance of an area of forest.

Developed world The name given to countries which are wealthy and where most people have comfortable lives.

Environment Air, water, soils and the animals and plants in one place.

Evolution The gradual change of animals and plants, often as a result of changes in their environment.

Extinct When an animal or plant species has died out forever.

Fossil fuels Fuels such as coal, oil or gas that are burnt to make energy.

Habitat The preferred home of particular animals and plants.

Incinerator A container that burns waste.

Mammal A warm-blooded animal with body hair.

Natural resources Materials which occur naturally in the world, such as wood, oil and water.

Ozone A layer of gas in the atmosphere which protects the Earth from the Sun's rays.

Pesticide A chemical used to kill animals and plants that cause damage to plants and crops.

Pollution Harmful substances released into the environment.

Solar panel A panel that can trap the energy from sunlight and convert it into electrical energy.

Species A group of animals or plants that look similar and which normally will only breed with each other.

Sustainable forest A type of forest where new trees are planted when the old ones are cut down.

INDEX *(Entries in **bold** refer to an illustration)*